My Dad the Magnificent

by Kristy Parker

illustrated by Lillian Hoban

DUTTON CHILDREN'S BOOKS • NEW YORK

Library of Congress Cataloging in Publication Data
Parker, Kristy.
  My dad the magnificent.
  Summary: Although Buddy might exaggerate a bit in
bragging about his magnificent father, the good times
they share demonstrate that his father really is great.
  [1. Fathers and sons—Fiction] I. Hoban, Lillian,
ill. II. Title.
PZ7.P2266My 1987 [E] 86-24077
ISBN 0-525-44314-2

Published in the United States by Dutton Children's Books,
375 Hudson Street, New York, N.Y. 10014
Editor: Ann Durell   Designer: Isabel Warren-Lynch
Printed in Hong Kong by South China Printing Co.
      COBE   10 9 8 7 6 5 4 3 2

for my dad, with love

My new friend Alex likes to brag.

Yesterday he started bragging about his dad. He told me that his dad was a fireman, and that once he rescued a little baby and a dog from a burning house.

I just had to tell Alex how great my dad is. So I did.

"Well," I said, "my dad is magnificent. On Mondays, he's a lion tamer. He snaps his whip, and the lions snarl. Then he says, 'Down, lions!' And the lions sit down because they know that when my dad says 'Down,' he means it."

"On Tuesdays, he's a cowboy. He jumps on his horse, Thunder, and he rides the range and rounds up wild cows."

"On Wednesdays, he plays pro basketball. He's the tallest one on the team. He leaps into the air for a slam-dunk, and *whoosh!* the ball goes right through the net. Everyone cheers."

"On Thursdays, he's a deep-sea diver. He dives deep into the ocean and digs up buried treasure. He even saved a little baby from a shark once."

"On Fridays, he's an explorer at the North Pole. He drives a sled pulled by eight white dogs. And he talks to Santa Claus. Santa Claus is my dad's best friend.

"And *that's* how magnificent my dad is," I said to Alex.

Then my dad came home from work. He said, "Hi, Buddy," the same way he does every day.

Alex wanted to know why he wasn't wearing his cowboy hat or his lion tamer's suit. He said he looked just like any ordinary dad to him.

So I had to tell Alex that I wasn't telling the truth. I had to tell him that my dad really wears a tie, and sits in his office and has meetings. Alex said he didn't think that was so great.

Then Alex said he had to go home. He said he'd see me tomorrow.

But I said, "I can't, Alex. Tomorrow's Saturday, and I always spend Saturdays with my dad."

Alex got this funny look on his face and rode off on his bike. I guess that didn't sound like much fun to him.

But on Saturdays, I see my dad all day. He fixes pancakes for breakfast and lets me put whipped cream on top.

After breakfast, he lifts me up in the air and lets me walk on the ceiling.

Then I help him wash the car. I do the tires because he says I'm a great tire washer.

He always tucks me in on Saturday nights. I brush my teeth, and he inspects them. He says, "Close your mouth before you hurt my eyes with those shiny teeth!"

Then he hugs me real tight, and he says, "I love you. See you in the morning."

And you know what? My dad is the most magnificent dad in the whole world. And that's the truth.